The Story of Adele H.

The Story

François Truffaut

of Adele H.

Edited by Helen C. Scott

English dialogue by Jan Dowson

Grove Press, Inc., New York

ISBN: 0-394-17908-0
Grove Press ISBN: 0-8021-4014-9
Library of Congress Catalog Card Number: 75-42798
First Evergreen Black Cat Edition 1976
First Printing 1976
Manufactured in the United States of America
Distributed by Random House, Inc., New York
GROVE PRESS, INC., 196 West Houston Street, New York, N.Y. 10014

This book is dedicated to
Frances Vernor Guille

Foreword

My desire to do a film about Adele Hugo dates back
to 1955, when I read her biography, written by
Frances Vernor Guille.

In 1968 I worked with my collaborator, Jean Gruault, to
adapt Jean Hugo's "Memoir" into the screen-
play of *The Wild Child*. I had been fascinated by the
creative process of using real-life events as the basis
for a fictional story that would not distort the authentic-
ity of the factual material. When it turned out that
Gruault shared my enthusiasm over Adele, I con-
vinced him and he agreed to our project at once.
But when I approached Jean Hugo, his initial reaction was one of reserve, if not downright reluctance:
to begin with, the story of his great-aunt was more or
less regarded as a skeleton in the family closet; besides, Jean Hugo was rather apprehensive about any
filmed impersonation of Victor Hugo.

Following our promise to spare him the sight of a
bearded actor claiming to be Victor Hugo and our
assurance that his great-grandfather would not be
represented on the screen, we got his permission to
go ahead with a first draft, to be submitted one year
later for his approval.

Meanwhile, working on the scenario of *Adele*
between each shooting, I completed three other films.

As soon as Jean Hugo approved our first draft, I asked Suzanne Schiffman to work on the final script with Gruault and myself. For while it is not easy to fashion an unanimist plot based on the criss-crossing actions of a dozen characters—as in *Day for Night*—it is almost as difficult to create an *intimiste* film, featuring a single personage.

And yet, I think that what really attracted me to this project was the solitary aspect of Adele's adventure. Having filmed love stories between two and three protagonists (*Jules and Jim*,) I felt it would be a fascinating challenge to concentrate on a single character, obsessed by a one-way passion.

The factors that appealed to me most in the story of Adele Hugo were:

1. Her story is the autopsy of a passion.
2. The girl is alone throughout the whole story.
3. She is the daughter of the most famous man in the world.
4. The man is referred to, but never seen.
5. Adele assumes a number of false identities.
6. Obsessed by her *idée fixe*, she pursues an unattainable goal.
7. Every word she utters and every move she makes is related to her fixation.
8. Though she fights a losing battle, Adele is continually active and inventive.

I am aware that everything one writes or films acquires a meaning. Nevertheless, I can truthfully say that in my creative process, the emotion is father to the theme.

Throughout the years, I have made some good films and some bad ones, but all were freely chosen. Adding them end to end, it is obvious that I am primarily concerned with the affective domain.

Curiously enough, I may discover, after the fact, through what others write about my work, the inner motivations that guided my choice of a given subject. Because I work instinctively rather than intellectually, it is often some two years after a film has been released that I fully understand its meaning.

This delayed insight is not necessarily a handicap. I would find it very uninspiring to go through the mechanical routine of shooting a film whose meaning has been predetermined.

By now, I am obviously aware that I have a predilection for films of sentiment, dealing with the painful and frustrating aspects of certain family and love relationships. Within each picture, I run into the conflict between temporary and definitive sentiments, so that I seem to be filming the same situations.

Those who have an affinity for these subjects—the low-key description of strong emotions—will see them as variants on a theme. Those who are bored with them will say that I repeat myself.

The Story of Adele H, which might be compared to a musical composition for a solo instrument, requires no further preliminary explanations. Suffice it to say that since I am obviously incapable of making films "against," I keep on filming "for."

Whether I am dealing with Antoine Doinel, Catherine, Montag, Julie, Muriel Brown, Victor of Aveyron, Camille Bliss, or Adele H, my love for each is the same.

FRANÇOIS TRUFFAUT

12

A Note on
Frances Vernor Guille

Frances Vernor Guille, a professor at Wooster College, in Ohio, was born in 1908, in Atlanta, Georgia. In 1949, she received a doctorate from the University of Paris.

The subject of Ms. Guille's doctoral thesis was François-Victor Hugo, one of the great poet's two sons. In the course of her research, Jean Hugo, the great-grandson of the poet, told her of the probable value of a misplaced diary kept by François-Victor's sister during the family's years of exile in the islands of Jersey and Guernsey. And so it was that Ms. Guille discovered Adele.

The Hugo family having accorded her the permission to read Adele's letters, Ms. Guille became increasingly interested in the young woman who followed her father in exile and then deserted him shortly afterward, to follow an English lieutenant, first to Nova Scotia and later to the island of Barbados.

In 1955, Ms. Guille discovered two volumes of Adele's diary in the Pierpont Morgan Library in New York City. In order to prepare the biography of Adele which would serve as the introduction to the first volume of her diary, Ms. Guille had to retrace, as it were, the young woman's tragic odyssey. *Le Journal d'Adele Hugo* was published in 1968 by Minard

(Lettres Modernes, Paris). One year later, François Truffaut read the book and conceived the idea of making a film on the subject.

In 1973, Ms. Guille married Walter Todd Secor, professor of French at the University of Denison, in Granville, Ohio.

Ms. Guille lived to see the first showing of *The Story of Adele H.* at the 13th New York Film Festival. She died a few days later, in October, 1975.

The Story of Adele H.

If everyone has heard of Leopoldine, the elder daughter of Victor Hugo, who was drowned with her husband at Villequier in 1843, the story of the poet's younger daughter—named Adele after her mother, and god-daughter of Saint-Beuve—is not generally known.

When Napoléon III came to power in the "coup d'Etat" of 1851, Adele went with her parents into exile in Jersey, and later, in Guernsey. It was she who was assigned the task of keeping "The Diary of Exile," while her brother, Charles, was busy translating Shakespeare, and her other brother François-Victor was learning the new art of photography.

An excellent musician, Adele left numerous scores in addition to a voluminous personal diary, written in code. Part of this diary has been found, painstakingly decoded, and published by Mrs. Frances Vernor Guille (Editions Minard).

It was at the beginning of the exile in Jersey, and later in Guernsey, that Adele made the acquaintance of a young English lieutenant, Albert Pinšon, who took part in several of the famous revolving table séances organized by Victor Hugo. Adele fell in love with the lieutenant, and abandoned Auguste Vacquerie who had hoped to marry her. (His brother Charles had married Leopoldine, and was drowned trying to save his young wife). At this moment, Adele was almost certainly Albert Pinson's mistress.

Was there ever any question of a marriage between Adele and the lieutenant? It is quite likely. But it is absolutely certain that the young man didn't give it a second thought when he set off with his regiment for Halifax, Nova Scotia, Canada. It was then that Adele fled from Guernsey, and set out to seek the man whom she considered as her "fiancé," in the hope of winning back his love.

The Story of Adele H, whose action begins in Halifax in 1863, when Adele arrives to try to reconquer the lieutenant, is the story of this unique and solitary love. It describes an obsession—that of marriage—in a young woman, who, at one and the same time, was proud of her father's fame, and anxious to change her own name. The same young woman who was keen to make her own existence, while struggling to recover from the shock of her sister Leopoldine's death, "the beloved of the whole family."

Credits

Production	LES FILMS DU CARROSSE LES ARTISTES ASSOCIÉS
Director	FRANÇOIS TRUFFAUT
Screenplay	FRANÇOIS TRUFFAUT, JEAN GRUAULT, SUZANNE SCHIFFMAN with the collaboration of FRANCES V. GUILLE, author of *Journal of Adele Hugo**
Music	MAURICE JAUBERT (1900–1940) orchestra conducted by PATRICE MESTRAL
Director of Photography	NESTOR ALMENDROS
English dialogue	JAN DOWSON

Technical:

Production Director	MARCEL BERBERT CLAUDE MILLER
1st Assistant Director	SUZANNE SCHIFFMAN
2nd Assistant Director	CARL HATHWELL

Production Manager	PATRICK MILLER
Property Master	DANIEL BRAUNSCHWEIG
Continuity	CHRISTINE PELLE
Sound Engineer	JEAN-PIERRE RUH
Set Decorator	JEAN-PIERRE KOHUT-SVELKO
Editor	YANN DEDET
Assistant Editor	MARTINE BARRAQUE-CURIE

*The film credits include an acknowledgment for the contribution of Carol McDaid Seib, who assisted Frances V. Guille in her work.

Cast

ADELE	ISABELLE ADJANI
LIEUTENANT PINSON	BRUCE ROBINSON
MRS. SAUNDERS, *the landlady*	SYLVIA MARRIOTT
MR. SAUNDERS	REUBIN DOREY*
MR. WHISTLER, *the bookseller*	JOSEPH BLATCHLEY
COLONEL WHITE	M. WHITE*
LIEUTENANT HATHWELL, *Pinson's orderly*	CARL HATHWELL*
THE HYPNOTIST	IVRY GITLIS*
MR. LENOIR, *the Notary*	SIR CECIL DE SAUSMAREZ*
JUDGE JOHNSTONE	SIR RAYMOND FALLA*
DR. MURDOCK	ROGER MARTIN*
MME BAA, *of Barbados*	MADAME LOUISE*
THE SCRIBE	JEAN-PIERRE LEURSSE*

*First screen appearance.

17

The Story of Adele H.

The cast and credits are superimposed over a series of striking, colored landscape drawings.[1]

As the screen blacks out, a caption appears: "The story of ADELE *is true. It is about events that really happened and people who really existed."*

As an antique map of America fills up the screen, the camera zooms in on Canada. Another more detailed map of Canada now appears. The continuing movement of the camera narrows in on Nova Scotia and then Halifax, as we hear the narration.

---

[1]These are reproductions of drawings made by Victor Hugo. The original drawings are on display in the Victor Hugo Museum, Place des Vosges, in Paris.

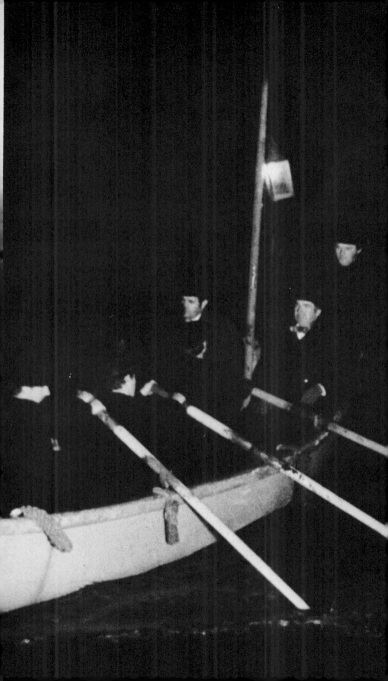

NARRATOR   The year is 1863. For two years now, the United States have been torn apart by the Civil War. Will Great Britain recognize the independence of the Southern Confederacy and join in the war against the Yankees? Since 1862, British troops have been stationed in the Canadian town of Halifax, capital of Nova Scotia, formerly known as French Acadia.[1] Halifax is charged with tension, as on the eve of a crisis. The feverish climate in the town is marked by carousing, illicit trafficking, and the hunt for Yankee spies.

A colored engraving of an incoming passenger ship appears on the screen.

NARRATOR   While down at the port, British authorities conduct a vigilant inspection of the European passengers disembarking from the *Great Eastern*, a huge steamship also known as "The Floating City."

---

[1] The population of Halifax is bilingual. Throughout the film, the characters will alternately speak in French or in English.

Port. Exterior. Night.

Among the passengers of the ship's boat nearing land is
ADELE. *We follow her as she gets off the boat and moves
about the pier. As she makes her way through the milling
crowd to a waiting coach, a noisy dispute is taking place
in the background between one of the passengers and a
suspicious British soldier, who insists on checking his pa-
pers.*

The coach, carrying ADELE *and her luggage, moves off
in the direction of the town.*

The Halifax Hotel. Exterior. Night.

*The coach comes to a halt in front of the hotel. We don't
see it, but the camera, which remains on* ADELE, *shows
that she is visibly disturbed by what she sees and hears.*

ADELE   Is this the hotel?

COACHMAN   This is it, Miss.

ADELE   No, no. I don't want to stay here.

COACHMAN   Apart from the Halifax, which is always
as full as this, there is only the Atlantic, which is
much too expensive. There is no hotel here fit for a
young lady. If you take my advice, you'll go to a
boardinghouse.

ADELE   Oh, yes! Please, please.

The vehicle rumbles off.

The Saunders' House. Exterior. Night.

A small house with a garden. On the wall, a sign reading

Room and Board. The coachman, whose name is O'BRIEN, *walks up to the door and knocks. A kindly looking woman opens the door.*

O'BRIEN   Good evening, Mrs. Saunders. I have a new lodger for you, a nice young lady.

MRS. SAUNDERS   Thank you, Mr. O'Brien.

O'BRIEN *walks back to* ADELE, *who is waiting in the carriage.*

O'BRIEN   We can go in, Miss.

ADELE   Thank you.

She gets out and walks to the house.

MRS. SAUNDERS   Let me take your case, Miss.

ADELE   Thank you. My name is Miss Lewly.

MRS. SAUNDERS   Come in, Miss Lewly.

After carrying her luggage into the house, O'BRIEN *takes his leave of* ADELE.

O'BRIEN   My name is O'Brien. I am always about if you want me.

ADELE   Thank you very much.

O'BRIEN   Goodnight, Miss.

ADELE'S ROOM. INTERIOR. NIGHT.

In a silent scene, we see ADELE, *lying in bed and looking thoughtful as she prepares to go to sleep.*

Fade out to black.

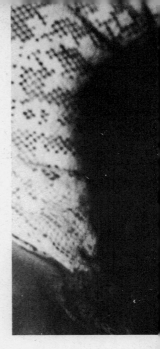

A. I

NOTAR

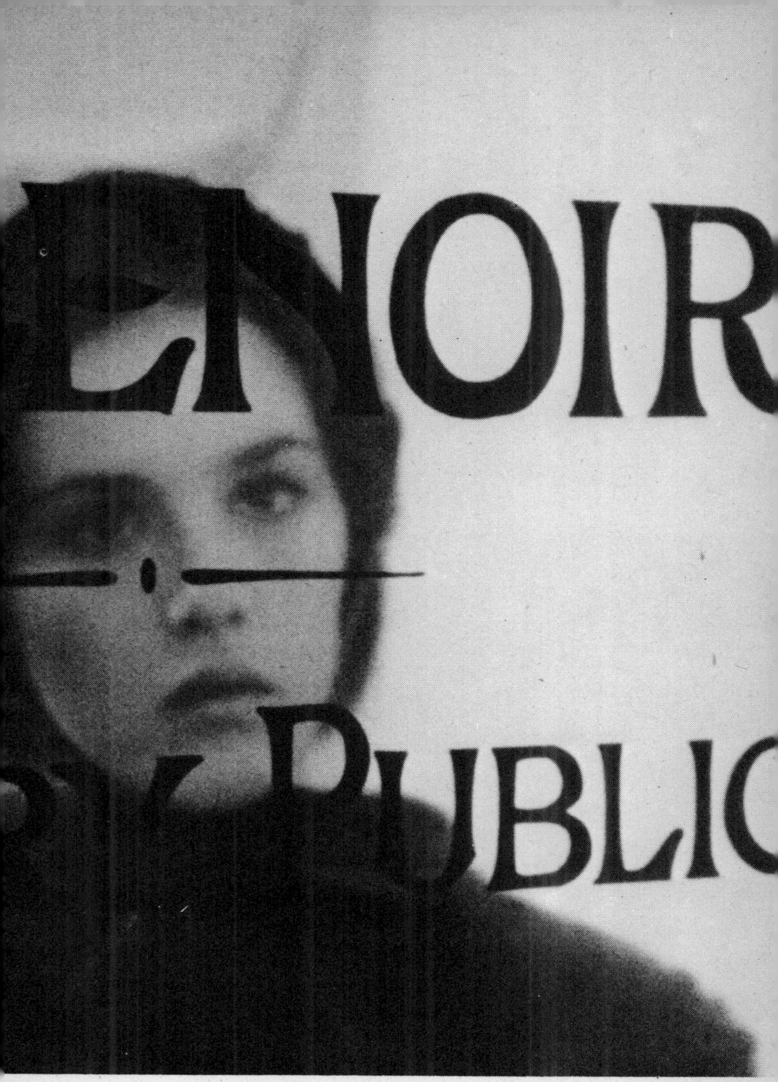

Notary Public's Office. Interior. Day.

The sign on the door reads : A. Lenoir, Notary Public. We see ADELE'S *image reflected in the glass as she waits for* MR. LENOIR *to open the door. The notary, elderly and courteous, is hard of hearing and uses an ear trumpet. During their conversation,[2]* ADELE *will occasionally repeat herself to make her meaning clear.*

ADELE   Good day, sir. My husband is a doctor. Dr. Lenormand of Paris. I've just arrived from France. I've been told you might help me.

LENOIR   That's good. I like France very much and will do my best to be of assistance. What is your problem?

ADELE   I have a niece in France. I'm very devoted to her. She is rather romantic. During a visit to England, she fell in love with a British officer, a Lieutenant Pinson, of the Sixteenth Hussars. There was even some talk of marriage between them. Our family was not really opposed to it. However, because of the troubles in America, Lieutenant Pinson was forced to leave suddenly with his regiment for Halifax. (*She repeats in a louder voice.*) For Halifax! Since then, we've had no news of him at all! My family wants me to look into the matter. It's very embarrassing . . . Lieutenant Pinson is of no interest to me. (*She repeats.*) I said Lieutenant Pinson is of no interest to me! I'm only concerned with my niece's happiness. That is all I can tell you.

LENOIR   Then you want me to find this Lieutenant . . .

ADELE   Pinson!

---

[2] This conversation is held in French.

The camera closes in on the notary as he sums up with a knowing smile:

LENOIR   . . . but in a discreet way.

WHISTLER'S BOOKSHOP. INTERIOR. DAY.

We notice ADELE *peering in through the window, as the bookshop owner is talking to a customer.*

WHISTLER   Yes, they all say so. Even the other officers tell me that we have a much better selection here than at the military library. Yet, we have far more problems with Customs than they do. In any case, I hope to have your books within a week . . . two at most.

As the customer makes his way to the door, we see he is a handsome young LIEUTENANT. *He is accompanied by a pretty young woman, carrying two lap dogs in her arms.*

LIEUTENANT   That's fine. Thanks.

WHISTLER   Goodbye, Lieutenant.

Outside the bookshop, ADELE *conceals herself while the* LIEUTENANT *and the young woman take their leave. As they walk over to their coach, she enters the bookshop.*[3]

WHISTLER   Good day, Madam. Can I help you?

ADELE   Yes, I'd like some paper.

WHISTLER   Some note paper?

ADELE   No, I need a whole ream . . . as for a memoir. I thought I recognized the officer who just left . . .

---

[3]The conversation between Adele and Mr. Whistler is in French.

She looks out at the coach which is moving off.

ADELE   Wasn't that Lieutenant Pinson?

WHISTLER   Yes, indeed. He's a good customer.

ADELE   I had no idea he was in Halifax.

WHISTLER   He hasn't been here very long, but he's already got quite a reputation as a man about town. Anyway, that's what they say.

ADELE   Really? What else do they say?

WHISTLER   To me, he's just another customer, you know. They also say he runs up debts. But here, he pays cash. Excuse me, Madam . . .

ADELE   Miss!

WHISTLER   Miss . . . is he related to you?

ADELE   Yes, he's my sister's brother-in-law. But I seldom see him since I'm not on good terms with my sister.

WHISTLER   I see.

ADELE   I'll take this.

WHISTLER   I also run a lending library by subscription, but you're welcome to use it even if you don't subscribe.

ADELE   Thank you. Goodbye.

THE SAUNDERS' HOME. INTERIOR. EVENING.

MR. SAUNDERS *is dressing up in a service livery, as* ADELE *enters the room.*

ADELE   Good evening, Mrs. Saunders.[4]

---

[4]Mrs. Saunders and Adele converse in French.

MRS. SAUNDERS   Miss Lewly, would you share my
   supper? My husband's helping out tonight as a
   waiter at the Officers' Club banquet.

ADELE *stops at the bottom of the stairs and turns back.
The camera stays on her throughout the scene.*

ADELE   Will the British officers be there?

MRS. SAUNDERS   Of course! The banquet is in honor
   of the Sixteenth Hussars Regiment!

ADELE   Then, my cousin should be there!

MRS. SAUNDERS   Do you have a cousin in Halifax?

ADELE   Yes. Lieutenant Pinson . . . That is, I call him
   my cousin, but we're not actually related. We were
   raised together. He is the son of the vicar in our
   village. To tell you the truth, he's been in love with
   me since we were children, though I've never en-
   couraged him. In any case, we haven't seen each
   other for years and this might be a good occasion
   to meet again. I could give you a letter for him, Mr.
   Saunders.

MR. SAUNDERS   Yes, of course.

ADELE   I'll write it now and bring it down. Just give
   me a few minutes.

ADELE *picks up an oil lamp and runs up the stairs.*

ADELE'S ROOM. INTERIOR. EVENING.

The camera closes up on ADELE's *face as she writes,
standing up at her escritoire:*

ADELE'S VOICE   Albert, my love,

Our separation destroyed me; I've thought of you every day since you left and I know you suffer as I do. I never received any of the letters you sent and am sure mine never reached you.

But now, I am here, Albert, on the same side of the ocean as you, and everything will be just as before. Soon, I will feel your arms around me. I am right nearby, Albert. I await you and I love you.

Your Adele

ADELE'S ROOM. INTERIOR. EVENING.

Later on that evening, MRS. SAUNDERS *is leafing through* ADELE's *picture album.*

MRS. SAUNDERS   The man who made these pictures is surely a very clever artist.

ADELE   He's my brother.

MRS. SAUNDERS   Well, do congratulate him. I've never seen such a remarkable likeness. It's as if you were alive.

MRS. SAUNDERS *turns the page to discover a drawing.*

MRS. SAUNDERS   Oh, what a lovely portrait. Is it you?

ADELE   No, it's my older sister.

MRS. SAUNDERS   Does she live in Europe?

ADELE   No, she died a long time ago.

MRS. SAUNDERS   Lord, I'm sorry.

ADELE   Leopoldine was drowned a few months after our mother made this portrait. She was nineteen and had just been married. They were out, boating. Her husband died with her. At the time, our father was on a journey, very far away. When he

learned the news by chance . . . from a newspaper, he nearly went mad with grief.

MRS. SAUNDERS What about you? You must have been very unhappy.

ADELE Leopoldine was everybody's favorite.

MRS. SAUNDERS How lovely she looks!

ADELE Her husband did everything he could to save her. When he realized she was lost, he chose to drown with her.

ADELE *takes a necklace from a bag of jewelry and shows it to* MRS. SAUNDERS.

ADELE This jewelry was hers. I always carry it with me.

MRS. SAUNDERS *takes the necklace and tries to put it on* ADELE, *who abruptly pulls back.*

ADELE No, no, I couldn't wear it!

MRS. SAUNDERS I understand, Miss Adele. You know, I've always wanted brothers and sisters.

ADELE No, you don't understand me. You don't know how lucky you are to be an only child!

MRS. SAUNDERS *is clearly dismayed by* ADELE's *vehemence.*

THE SAUNDERS' PARLOR. INTERIOR. NIGHT.

MR. SAUNDERS *comes home. The two women are seated at the table.*

MRS. SAUNDERS *helps her husband take his coat off.*

MR. SAUNDERS   Oh, sweetheart, I thought it would never end.

MRS. SAUNDERS   You must be tired.

MR. SAUNDERS   Yes, and wet! I saw your cousin, Miss Lewly.

ADELE   You saw him?

MR. SAUNDERS   Yes.

ADELE   How did he look?

MR. SAUNDERS   Well, he was dressed up to the nines. They'd never seen anybody looking so elegant.

ADELE   What did he talk about? Did you hear what he was saying?

MR. SAUNDERS   He told funny stories . . . really funny ones. He had them all laughing . . . Even the footmen were in stitches.

MRS. SAUNDERS   And the letter? Did you give the letter to Miss Lewly's cousin?

MR. SAUNDERS   Yes, of course I did.

MRS. SAUNDERS   Then, what are you waiting for? Give Miss Adele the reply.

MR. SAUNDERS   Well . . . there was no reply. The lieutenant read the letter, but didn't want to answer it.

ADELE   Oh, that doesn't matter. I didn't really expect a reply.

During this conversation, the camera has gradually moved in on ADELE, *now revealing an expression of distress that belies her casual remark.*

MRS. SAUNDERS   What was there on the menu?

MR. SAUNDERS   It was General Doylee's chef—you

know the one—who thought up the menu. There was turtle soup, curried chicken . . .

ADÈLE leaves the table to return to her room. As she walks upstairs, we continue to hear the description of the menu.

MR. SAUNDERS . . . salmon with scallions, venison steaks *au piment*, *filet de sole* in truffle sauce, artichokes with peppers, and Scotch grouse in whiskey. Raspberry ice and savories . . . the whole lot . . .

The camera now moves back to the SAUNDERS couple. As soon as they hear the sound of the door upstairs closing, MR. SAUNDERS leans over to his wife and whispers.

MR. SAUNDERS That letter, you know . . . the lieutenant didn't even open it. He just looked at the envelope, shrugged his shoulders, and stuffed it into his pocket without reading it. For a man in love, that's a funny way to behave.

Fade out to black.

ADELE'S ROOM. INTERIOR. NIGHT.

ADELE, in bed, is having a violent nightmare. As she tosses back and forth in anguish, a superimposed image appears on the screen, showing her in a desperate struggle to save herself from drowning. ADELE wakes up, screaming.

Fade out to black.

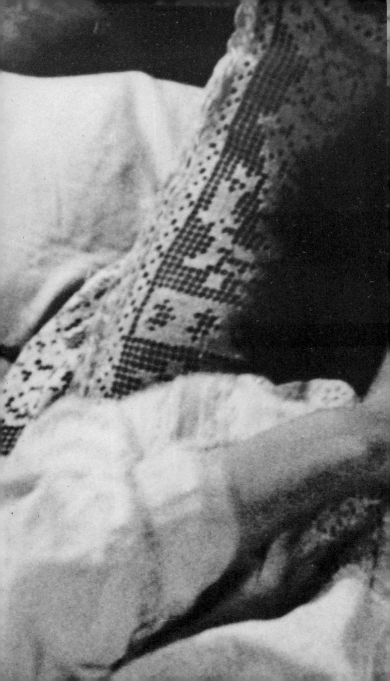

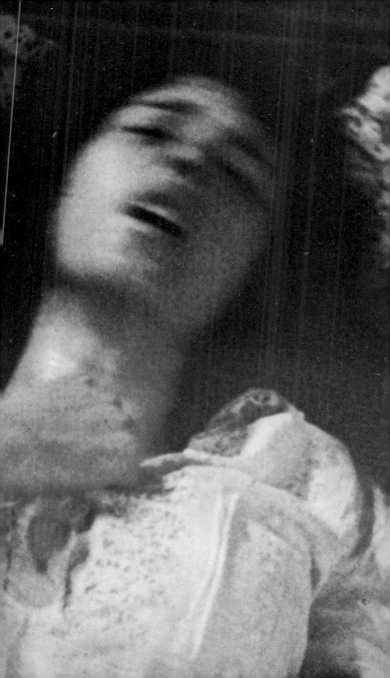

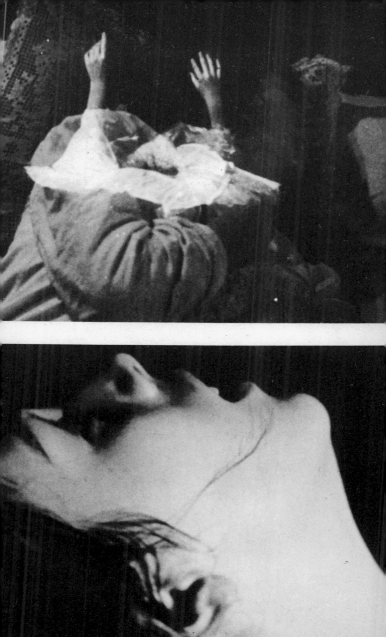

THE HALIFAX BANK. EXTERIOR AND INTERIOR. DAY.

O'BRIEN's coach pulls up to the door and ADELE gets out. She goes up to one of the counters. In response to her question, the clerk hands her a letter. After reading it, she says she is also expecting a money order. She is visibly disappointed when the clerk explains that it will probably take another two weeks to arrive.

ADELE'S ROOM. INTERIOR. DAY.

ADELE folds and then cuts the large sheet of paper to letter-size. As she writes, she reads out loud.

ADELE'S VOICE   My dear parents,
If I left without warning, it was to avoid another one of those discussions which even the simplest things seem to provoke in our family. If Lieutenant Pinson was to leave his post now, he would jeopard-ize his whole career. Therefore, I cannot leave him now. As you know, I love him as he loves me. We wish to be married. However, I will do nothing without your consent and expect a reply from you both.
With fondest love.

Adele.

P.S. Father owes me two months' allowance for May and June. I know that part of the money is being forwarded through the British Bank of North America, but I shall certainly need the full amount as life in Halifax is very expensive.

Fade out to black.

HALIFAX RAMPARTS. EXTERIOR. DAY.

ADELE *is strolling alongside the ramparts. As an officer passes her, she suddenly turns around, hurries to catch up with him, and taps him on the shoulder. The officer stops and gives the girl a blank, questioning look.[5] From her disconcerted reaction, we understand she has mistaken him for* PINSON. *She moves away.*

ADELE'S ROOM. INTERIOR. NIGHT.

ADELE *is seated at her table. From what we hear, we gather she is writing her diary.*

ADELE'S VOICE   We must regard the small things in life as if they are important. I know that moral battles are waged alone. Thousands of miles away from my family, I look at life differently. I can learn everything by myself, but for love, I need him. When we meet, I will tell him: "If one of us doesn't love enough to want marriage above all else, then it isn't love."
He has often reproached me for the violence of my emotions. When life brings us together again, I am determined to do nothing that might frighten him. I shall win him over by my gentleness . . . by my gentleness.

Fade out to black.

HALIFAX BANK. INTERIOR AND EXTERIOR. DAY.

ADELE *walks up to the clerk we have seen previously. He hands her a money order and directs her to the cashier's*

---

[5]We recognize François Truffaut in the role of the officer.

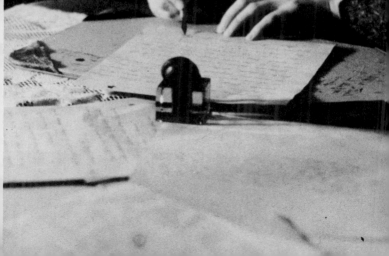

window. ADELE *collects her money, goes outside, and steps into the waiting coach, instructing* O'BRIEN *to take her home.*

Fade out to black.

THE SAUNDERS' PARLOR. INTERIOR. DAY.

In response to a knock, MRS. SAUNDERS *opens the door. We recognize* PINSON.

PINSON   I'd like to speak to the young lady who lives here.

MRS. SAUNDERS   Oh, Miss Lewly. Yes, she'll be so . . . What name shall I say?

PINSON   Tell her it's her friend from Guernsey.

MRS. SAUNDERS   From Guernsey? Yes, come in, sir. Please.

MRS. SAUNDERS *runs up the stairs and knocks on* ADELE's *door.*

MRS. SAUNDERS   Miss Lewly, Miss Lewly. There's a visitor to see you.

ADELE   Who is it?

MRS. SAUNDERS   I think it's him . . . the lieutenant!

ADELE   I'll be right down!

ADELE'S ROOM. INTERIOR. DAY.

Visibly torn between happiness and panic, ADELE *presses her hand to her face and looks at herself in the mirror.*

THE SAUNDERS' PARLOR. INTERIOR. DAY.

MRS. SAUNDERS informs PINSON that ADELE will be right down and urges him to make himself comfortable as she goes on with her ironing.

MRS. SAUNDERS   You're Lieutenant Pinson, I believe.

PINSON   Yes.

MRS. SAUNDERS   It's a long time, isn't it, since you saw Miss Lewly?

PINSON   Yes, it is.

MRS. SAUNDERS   One could hardly say that your cousin is a very cheerful young lady, but the house is so much more lively since she's here. Oh yes, we love having her with us. You can see at once that she is refined and well-educated. And she's so pretty. She has such beautiful eyes. Yes sir, she is going to be pleased to see you!

ADELE'S ROOM. INTERIOR. DAY.

Trying to decide what to wear, ADELE conducts a frantic search through the closet, throwing several dresses on her bed.

THE SAUNDERS' PARLOR. INTERIOR. DAY.

PINSON, standing by the window, is visibly losing patience.

PINSON   I'm sorry. I'll have to go. I'm on duty.

MRS. SAUNDERS   Please wait, she will only be a minute.

PINSON   I'm sorry. I don't have time.

PINSON *moves toward the door. Just as he is about to leave,* ADELE, *looking quite beautiful in an elegant blue dress, comes down the stairs and calls out to him.*

ADELE   Albert!

As he stops, she gives her landlady a meaningful look. MRS. SAUNDERS *leaves the room. Alone with* PINSON, ADELE *goes up to him and presses her hand to his lips, as if to keep him from talking.*

ADELE   At last!

PINSON   You cannot remain here. You should not have come.

ADELE   I'll go where you wish, my love. I will obey you in every way. I belong to you. Do with me whatever you will. I love you so much!

PINSON   Adele, I'm sure you've run away. You are here without your family's permission, aren't you?

ADELE   That's not true: they know I'm in Halifax. I wrote my father.

PINSON   And what did the great man say? I'm certain you left without telling him. Am I right?

ADELE   I told him I was going to Malta, but then I wrote him from New York.

PINSON   Malta! Adele, you say you will obey me. I want you to go back to Guernsey. Your family must be worried about you. Think of your father . . . of his reputation. Besides, you must not pursue me!

ADELE   Albert, it can all be arranged: when I marry I shall receive forty thousand francs. I will dispose of two thousand francs a year. My family has no right to tell me how to spend the money. Besides, my father and mother have now given their consent to our marriage.

PINSON   I don't believe you. Show me their formal consent.

ADELE   I will show it to you.

PINSON   You haven't got it. I knew it! Your father has always despised me. In any case, I haven't come to propose, but to ask you to leave Halifax.

ADELE *pulls a letter from the bodice of her dress and hands it to* PINSON.

ADELE   Look at this!
PINSON   What is it?

He reads it.

PINSON   I don't understand.
ADELE   It's a proposal of marriage from Canizario!
PINSON   Who is he?
ADELE   A friend of my father's . . . a great Italian poet.
PINSON   Well then, marry him.
ADELE   But, it's you I'm in love with. Don't you love me any more, Albert? Do you still love me now?
PINSON   I did love you, Adele.
ADELE   Could you love me again? You don't answer. Then all I ask is that you let me love you. Please, let me love you!

ADELE *takes a few steps away. Then, in an abrupt change of mood, she turns around and cries out in a shrill voice.*

ADELE   I warn you: if you reject me, I will go to your
superiors! I will show them your letters! I will de-
stroy you! I will denounce you and have you
thrown out of the army!

PINSON *shrugs his shoulders and prepares to leave. In
another about-face,* ADELE *rushes to the door. With tears
in her eyes, she pleads with him.*

ADELE   Please, don't go!

She presses a roll of bills upon him.

PINSON   What's this?
ADELE   For your gambling debts.
PINSON   I'd need ten times as much for my debts.
ADELE   Keep it anyway. I beg you!

After hesitating for a moment, he takes the money.

PINSON   All right, I accept it. But not as a present,
just as a loan!
ADELE   Just as you wish, my love. Will you come
back? If you like, I can come to you . . . whenever
you like, wherever you like.

PINSON *tears himself out of her embrace and closes the
door behind him. For a moment,* ADELE, *still agitated,
leans against the door.*

ADELE'S ROOM. INTERIOR. DAY.

A slow traveling forward on ADELE. *Seated at her table,
she is writing to* PINSON.

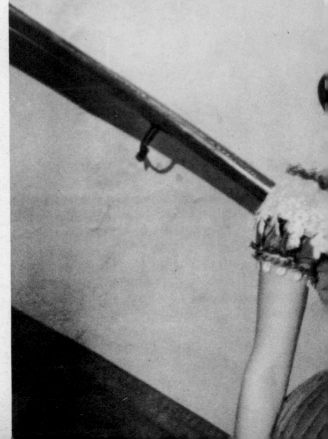

ADELE'S VOICE   My love,

I'm so happy we have found each other again. Your absence was sheer agony. We shall not allow any more misunderstanding to come between us. I knew you couldn't forget me. When a woman like me gives herself to a man, she is his wife. I'll weep no more. One can no more exchange one's father, mother, or children, than one's wife or husband. I am your wife forever more, till death do us part.

Slow fade out to black.

THE SAUNDERS' BEDROOM. INTERIOR. NIGHT.

As they hear strange sounds from the room above, the SAUNDERS *couple exchange a look of compassion.*

MRS. SAUNDERS   The poor child!

ADELE'S ROOM. INTERIOR. NIGHT.

ADELE is seated at a small, round table, her hands extended slightly above the surface; she stares straight ahead. As if in response to a voice only she can hear, she whispers:

ADELE   Are you there, Leopoldine? Leopoldine, I know you are there. You must help me!

A HOUSE. EXTERIOR. NIGHT.

A coach pulls up in front of the house. PINSON *gets out, goes to the door, and rings. The woman we have seen with*

*him at the bookshop opens the door. The two exchange a
loving kiss before going in.*

A little further down the road, a second coach stops and
ADELE *gets out. Moving stealthily through the foliage,
she makes her way to a vantage point from which she can
observe the couple inside going up the stairs and the two
lap dogs come tumbling down. Now, having scaled a tool
shed, she has a clear view of the couple in the bedroom. As
she watches them making love, a strange smile steals over*
ADELE's *face.*

Fade out to black.

ADELE'S ROOM. INTERIOR. NIGHT.

Fade in on ADELE, *who is writing.*

ADELE'S VOICE   I am beyond pride and jealousy.
Since love will not smile at me, I submit to its
grimace. I want to think now, of my sisters who
suffer in bordellos and my sisters who suffer in
marriage.

*Having reached the bottom of the page, she looks around.
Realizing there is no more writing paper, she hastily tears
two blank pages out of the nearest book and resumes her
feverish scribbling.*

ADELE'S VOICE   They must be given liberty, dignity, a
mind of their own, and a heart to love with. Love is
my religion. I can no more give my body without
my soul than I can give my soul without my body.
Despite my youth, I sometimes feel I am in the
autumn of my life.

Whistler's Bookshop. Interior. Day.

The falling snow we see through the window indicates that we are now in winter. The passage of time is also evident from the deterioration in ADELE's *appearance as she enters the shop: pale and disheveled, she is shivering with cold. Noticing the change in the young woman,* WHISTLER *is visibly concerned.*

WHISTLER   Ah, Miss Lewly . . . You should be wearing a coat in this weather. I'll get you a warm drink . . . a nice grog.

ADELE   No, thanks, I have no time. I just want some paper.

WHISTLER   How many reams?

ADELE   I need two reams.

WHISTLER   Just this morning, I was thinking that you might be in today, since you didn't come last week. I said to myself: the young lady generally comes in on Wednesdays. Still, in weather like this, most people prefer to stay home. Anyway, I put them aside . . . just in case.

ADELE   Thank you, Mr. Whistler.

WHISTLER   So you remember my name? It's easy for me to remember you: there are very few people who write as much as you do . . . especially in Halifax. You must excuse me for babbling away. Here's the paper.

ADELE   Oh, I'm sorry. I don't have enough money with me for both. Just give me one ream.

WHISTLER   Oh, no! Take them both. You'll pay me some other time.

ADELE   No, I don't want to.

WHISTLER   It's my pleasure!

ADELE   Thank you. Goodbye, Mr. Whistler.

WHISTLER   Goodbye, Miss Lewly.

Through the window, WHISTLER watches ADELE walk away. Suddenly, she staggers and collapses in the street. A small crowd gathers around her. WHISTLER rushes out and, with a few passers-by, helps her into O'BRIEN's coach. Muttering to himself, he hurries back to lock his shop in order to accompany the sick girl.

THE SAUNDERS' PARLOR. INTERIOR. DAY.

In response to a knock at the door, MRS. SAUNDERS walks over to open it to WHISTLER. He has a package in his arms.

MRS. SAUNDERS   Ah, Mr. Whistler. Do come in.

WHISTLER   Good afternoon, Mrs. Saunders. I came to . . . How is Miss Lewly's health?

MRS. SAUNDERS   Well, she's better, but she's still in her room.

WHISTLER   Ah yes, I thought . . . this is the paper she usually takes. She must have run out by now. Well . . . thank you.

MRS. SAUNDERS   Oh, don't go! Wait a minute. I'll tell her you're here. She'll be so pleased to see you.

WHISTLER   Ah, yes. Fine.

The camera stays on WHISTLER as MRS. SAUNDERS goes upstairs to ask whether ADELE will see him. A few minutes later, she comes down.

90

MRS. SAUNDERS Miss Adele thanks you very much for the paper, but she's too tired to see anyone.

WHISTLER Never mind. I was only passing by and I thought she might like . . .

MRS. SAUNDERS Of course. Thank you.

WHISTLER It doesn't matter. I'm so sorry to trouble you. Goodbye, Mrs. Saunders.

MRS. SAUNDERS Goodbye, Mr. Whistler. Thank you.

ADELE'S ROOM. INTERIOR. DAY.

Propped up against the pillows of a daybed, ADELE *is writing a letter. Through the window, we see the falling snow.*

ADELE'S VOICE My dear parents,
I am desperate: Mr. Pinson will only marry me on condition he receives a written consent from both of you to our marriage. I am practically penniless: it is impossible to live in Halifax for less than four hundred francs a month. I find it unbearable to owe money to the people I am staying with. My health is fine. My love to you all.
P.S. Don't forget to give me news of my music album. Have you sent it to the publishers?

MRS. SAUNDERS *knocks and walks into the half-open door to announce that* DR. MURDOCK *has arrived. As she is leaving,* ADELE *calls her back and hands her the envelope.*

ADELE Could your husband mail this letter for me? I want it posted today.

MRS. SAUNDERS *takes the envelope, ushers the doctor in, and introduces him to his patient. He walks over to the bed and sits down by* ADELE's *side.*

DR. MURDOCK   May I have your hand, please?

ADELE   Of course.

THE SAUNDERS' PARLOR. INTERIOR. DAY.

Through a door, we see MRS. SAUNDERS *working in the kitchen. As the* DOCTOR *comes down the stairs, she joins him in the parlor.*

MRS. SAUNDERS   How is she, Doctor?

DR. MURDOCK   Well, it's a little more serious than a simple chill. There is a touch of pleurisy. She needs looking after.

MRS. SAUNDERS   Oh, she'll be well looked after, Doctor. I promise you.

DR. MURDOCK   Yes, but our patient seems rather headstrong and recovery may be long. Two or three weeks . . . perhaps longer. Ah, if only spring would come!

MRS. SAUNDERS   Doctor, could you post this letter for me?

DR. MURDOCK   Of course.

MRS. SAUNDERS   Normally, I'd have asked Mr. Saunders to post it, but he won't be in until late.

Taking the envelope from her hand, the doctor casts an automatic glance at it and looks up in surprise as he reads

the address: Monsieur Victor Hugo, Hauteville House, Guernsey (Channel Islands).

DR. MURDOCK   Who in this house can be writing letters to Victor Hugo?

MRS. SAUNDERS   Miss Lewly.

DR. MURDOCK   Miss Lewly! What do you know of this young lady?

MRS. SAUNDERS   Well, she hasn't told me very much about herself, but I know she is French. She did tell me her sister was drowned at the age of nineteen.

DR. MURDOCK   Drowned at nineteen? That's Leopoldine! Do you realize that your lodger is the second daughter of Victor Hugo?

MRS. SAUNDERS   But . . . this Victor Hugo . . .

DR. MURDOCK   Why, Victor Hugo is the greatest living poet! Like Homer . . . Dante . . . Shakespeare! He's also a political figure who was persecuted for his ideas. At the risk of his life, he opposed the *coup d'etat* which overthrew the French Republic. His two sons were imprisoned and he had to seek refuge in Brussels. He now lives in Guernsey, a little island between the coasts of France and Britain.

MRS. SAUNDERS   She did tell me about that island.

DR. MURDOCK   I assure you, Madam, the man is a genius! Incredible! Well, I'm very proud to have examined this young woman. Do you realize, Mrs. Saunders, that your lodger is the daughter of the most famous man in the world? Do you think we should tell her that we know who she is?

MRS. SAUNDERS   Oh, no, Doctor! If Miss Adele is hiding under an assumed name, she must have a very good reason for doing so. She's an honest person, incapable of doing any wrong. If she wants to conceal her identity, we must respect her wishes.

DR. MURDOCK You're quite right, we will keep this to ourselves.

MRS. SAUNDERS Just a moment. I want to make a note of that address. We never know.

She sits down and copies the address in her notebook.

Fade out to black.

ADELE'S ROOM. INTERIOR. NIGHT.

Drenched in perspiration and gasping for breath, ADELE *is having another nightmare. An image superimposed over her feverish agitation shows her thrashing around in the water, to keep from drowning.*

Fade out to black.

GARRISON. EXTERIOR. DAY.

In her obsessive pursuit of PINSON, ADELE *has managed to gain access to the garrison grounds. As a group of soldiers marches by, she furtively conceals herself behind a wall.*

PINSON'S QUARTERS. INTERIOR. DAY.

As he is putting on his uniform, PINSON *is surprised to discover a note in one of the pockets. Continuing his*

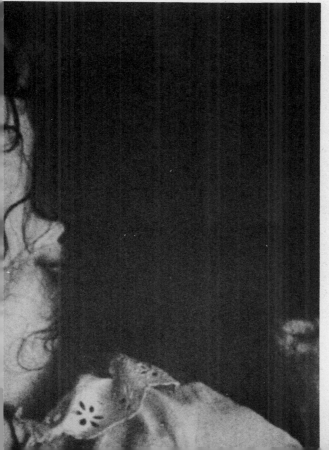

search, he finds several others. We hear ADELE'S *voice, as he reads them one by one.*

ADELE *(off-camera)*   Remember to think of me.
I tremble with love. Do not reject me.
I am not me without you.
At this moment, I don't love you.
It is too difficult to keep our secret.
Don't be surprised if you find me roaming the streets, crying out my love for you.

Opening his door, PINSON *calls out for his orderly.*

PINSON   Hathwell!

HATHWELL   Yes, sir?

PINSON   Where was this coat cleaned?

HATHWELL   At the usual place, sir.

PINSON   Did anybody touch it?

HATHWELL   Not that I know of, sir.

PINSON   All right, thank you.

Halifax Bank. Interior. Day.

Once again, ADELE *is talking to the same clerk. He hands her an envelope. Turning around, she notices a* CHILD, *a little boy, hiding under a counter, and goes over to him.*

ADELE   What are you doing? What's your name?

CHILD   David.

ADELE   David. That's a lovely name.

CHILD   What's your name?

ADELE   Mine? Mine is Leopoldine.

She moves to the side, opens the envelope, and we hear what she reads.

ADELE'S VOICE   Your mother is very ill. When you write to her, remember that she can only make out large handwriting. I'm sending you a money order for seven hundred francs through the Halifax Bank, as well as both of our consents to your marriage.

ADELE now unfolds a second sheet of paper. As she reads, we hear a male voice.

VICTOR HUGO'S VOICE   I, Victor Hugo, former peer of France, hereby authorize my daughter to marry . . .

ADELE goes back to the letter.

ADELE'S VOICE   But I warn you, Adele, and this is my final word on the matter: either you get married immediately, or you come right home.

ADELE walks back to the CHILD.

ADELE   I lied to you. My real name is Adele.

As she walks toward the door, we remain on the CHILD, staring after the strange young woman.

MANSION. EXTERIOR. NIGHT.

A slight male figure, dressed in tails and a high hat,

jumps over the wall, into the garden leading to a brightly lit mansion. From the strains of the orchestra and the elegant couples strolling about, we gather that a fancy ball is taking place inside. As the intruder emerges from the darkness, and moves toward the house, we recognize ADELE. *We now see her questioning a man who points to an orderly standing inside, near the door.* ADELE *goes up to him.*

They exchange a few words and she hands him a note. The orderly goes upstairs, where PINSON *is enjoying a conversation with a beautiful woman, and gives him the note.* PINSON *goes down to find* ADELE *waiting for him at the foot of the stairs. Grabbing her by the arm, he drags her away from the mansion.*

Except for the sound of the music, the whole scene is played out in silence.

CEMETERY. EXTERIOR. NIGHT.

The strains of the dance music in the distance contrast with the stark setting of the graveyard. As PINSON *pulls the girl's hat off with an angry gesture, her hair tumbles down around her shoulders.*

PINSON   I don't understand you, Adele. What are you doing here? You disguise yourself to spy on me now?

ADELE   Not at all! I dressed this way so as not to embarrass you.

PINSON   How considerate! Thank you.

PINSON *moves away from her. Ignoring his sarcasm,* ADELE *tries to reason with him.*

ADELE   Albert, I absolutely had to see you!

She hands him a letter.

ADELE   Look, I have received my parents' agreement.

PINSON   So your father's changed his mind, has he? I wouldn't have believed it.

ADELE   You see, we can be married now.

PINSON   I've already told you, Adele, it's out of the question.

ADELE   How you've changed, Albert. Have you forgotten the letters you wrote? I haven't. In some of them, you mention marriage. I could show them to all your women. Albert, you haven't forgotten what you wrote?

PINSON   All right, it's true. I did consider marrying you at one time, but now I don't. What harm is there in that?

At these words, ADELE *becomes indignant.*

ADELE   What harm? Albert, I didn't start this. You were the one who pursued me! You were the one who wanted me! You were the one who furtively reached for my arm at the séances . . . who caressed me in the corridors! I gave myself to you. Now, you've got to keep me!

PINSON   You can't be serious: I had women before I met you and I've had women since you. I intend to have others in the future.

ADELE   But you'll be just as free after we're married. You can have as many women as you want.

109

Still trying to win him over, ADELE *now tries a different approach.*

ADELE   You know, I saw you with that woman and her dogs. She looks charming. Did you tell her about me?

PINSON   There are times when I wonder what goes on in your mind.

ADELE   How I wish we could be as we were in London . . . when we used to meet in secret.

Suddenly, she turns on PINSON *and lashes out at him, in a fury.*

ADELE   I gave up everything for you! I rejected my parents . . . I broke off with a man who wanted to marry me . . . the only man who really loved me!

PINSON   Be careful, Adele, I won't be blackmailed.

ADELE   I love you! Is it so hard to understand that I love you?

PINSON   If you loved me in a truly unselfish way, you wouldn't try to force me to marry you. When you love someone, you want him to be free. If you really love me, you will leave Halifax and go back to Guernsey.

ADELE *pauses to regain her composure. Seemingly resigned, she moves over to where* PINSON *is standing to make a final appeal.*

ADELE   Just say that you love me.

PINSON   Adele . . .

ADELE   I will go away and won't try to see you again. But before we part forever, I just want to ask whether you could still love me.

As PINSON *hesitates, she puts her arms around him.*

ADELE   Kiss me!

He leans over to kiss her on the forehead, but she raises her head and kisses him on the lips.

Fade out to black.

ADELE'S ROOM. INTERIOR. NIGHT.

A letter is lying on the table. ADELE *is kneeling in front of a chest of drawers that has been fashioned into an altar, with a bunch of flowers and a lighted candle on either side. Her hands clasped and her head raised,* ADELE *seems to be praying. In the center of the wall, we now discover the object of her worship: a framed picture of* PINSON. *As the camera moves in on her, we see a single tear streaming down her cheek.*

An overprint of ADELE's *face, while the camera now travels some thousand miles, over heaving ocean waves, to a map of Nova Scotia, which recedes to make way for the coastal line of France, gradually closing in on the Island of Guernsey.*

On these images, we hear ADELE *reading her letter.*

ADELE'S VOICE   My dear parents,
I have just married Lieutenant Pinson. The ceremony took place on Saturday, in a Halifax church. I must have money for my trousseau. In addition to my allowance, I need three hundred francs immediately. I've asked you a hundred times to have my music published. If you had done what I asked,

I wouldn't have to behave like a beggar. In the future, you will address me as follows: "Madame Pinson, 33 North Street, Halifax, Nova Scotia." Be sure to spell out "Madame" very clearly on the address.

I hope my good news reaches you rapidly.

HAUTEVILLE HOUSE. EXTERIOR. DAY.

The camera now pans down on the residence of VICTOR HUGO *in Guernsey. A group of curiosity-seekers stands in front of the house. The door opens to make way for an elderly woman, obviously a servant. In reply to a question, she informs the crowd that* VICTOR HUGO *is too ill to come out. We follow her as she makes her way toward the building of the* Guernsey Press. *Inside, she asks to speak to the* EDITOR *and hands him a letter.*

SERVANT   Monsieur Victor Hugo wishes to put an announcement in your paper.

The EDITOR *reads the letter.*

EDITOR   So, Victor Hugo's daughter has married an Englishman.

SERVANT   Yes, Lieutenant Pinson!

Fade out to black.

GARRISON. EXTERIOR. NIGHTFALL.

An officer is walking through the grounds as the soldiers stand at attention.

Colonel's Office. Interior. Day.

As PINSON *reaches the door, an officer comes out and informs him the* COLONEL *is expecting him.* PINSON *enters, and through the half-open door, we see him standing at attention. We do not see the* COLONEL, *but hear his voice as he sarcastically berates his subordinate.*

COLONEL *(off-camera)*   Ah, Pinson. Listen to this: "Married in Paris on September 17th: Mr. Albert Pinson, of the Sixteenth English Hussars, who fought with distinction in the Crimean War: to Mademoiselle Adele Hugo, daughter of Victor Hugo, one-time peer of France and former people's representative under the Republic, member of the Académie Française and Knight of the Order of Charles III of Spain, domiciled in St. Peter Port, Guernsey." Well, Pinson, so you've become ubiquitous, have you?

The COLONEL *now comes into view, circling around* PINSON *as he continues to admonish him.*

COLONEL   While you're here, drilling in Halifax, your double is off in Paris, marrying Victor Hugo's daughter. And where did you fight the Crimean War? In Baden-Baden, or in Monte-Carlo?

PINSON   Colonel, I assure you, this is some kind of a joke! It's true, I often visited the Hugo family in exile. Miss Hugo is a high-strung young lady. I did hear that she'd left her father's house, but I've no idea where she is now. And I give you my word of honor as an officer that I had nothing whatsoever to do with this announcement.

COLONEL   Come to the point. Are you married, or aren't you?

PINSON   No, Colonel, I am not married!

COLONEL   I'm prepared to believe you, but if your behavior were beyond reproach, you would not be exposed to mishaps of this kind. You will do me the pleasure of clearing up this misunderstanding without delay. One more escapade, and I shall have you brought before a court-martial! Very well, you are dismissed!

Fade out to black.

HALIFAX BANK. INTERIOR. DAY.

The clerk hands a letter to ADELE *who moves over to a corner to read it.*

VICTOR HUGO'S VOICE   Adele,
We are very disappointed by your behavior. You deceived us. You are not married and there is no hope you will ever be. Mr. Pinson has written to us, stating clearly that he will never marry you. Your mother wanted to go to Halifax to bring you home. It was very difficult to dissuade her. Such a journey might be fatal, as her health is getting worse every day. I'm sending you six hundred francs for your fare home. If you decide to return, your brother will await you in Liverpool.
I kiss you with all my heart. Adele, think of your mother, think of us. Come home.

ADELE *walks over to a counter and signs a receipt for the money order.*

Fade out to black.

ADELE'S ROOM. INTERIOR. NIGHT.

In bed, propped up against some pillows, ADELE *is visibly tense as she writes a reply to her father.*

ADELE'S VOICE   My dear parents,
You are right, I am not married to Lieutenant Pinson. He broke his word despite his many proposals of marriage. I keep his letters locked up in a special chest I had made. I don't agree with your idea to sue him for breach of promise, or to demand damages. If you wish, you could write him to point out how happy you would be to welcome him into our family. And tell him that he will never find a more loving wife.
I love my mother and father and my brothers. I love you all. But no power on earth can make me leave Halifax as long as he's here.

Fade out to black.

WHISTLER'S BOOKSHOP. INTERIOR. DAY.

WHISTLER *goes over to* ADELE *who is browsing through the bookshelves.*

WHISTLER   Miss, I have a package for you. It's a present. I put it aside some time ago, but wasn't sure I should give it to you. Here it is.

ADELE   For me?

WHISTLER   Yes, open it. I'll wrap it up again later.

WHISTLER *stands by timidly as* ADELE, *smiling in anticipation, unwraps the package which contains three*

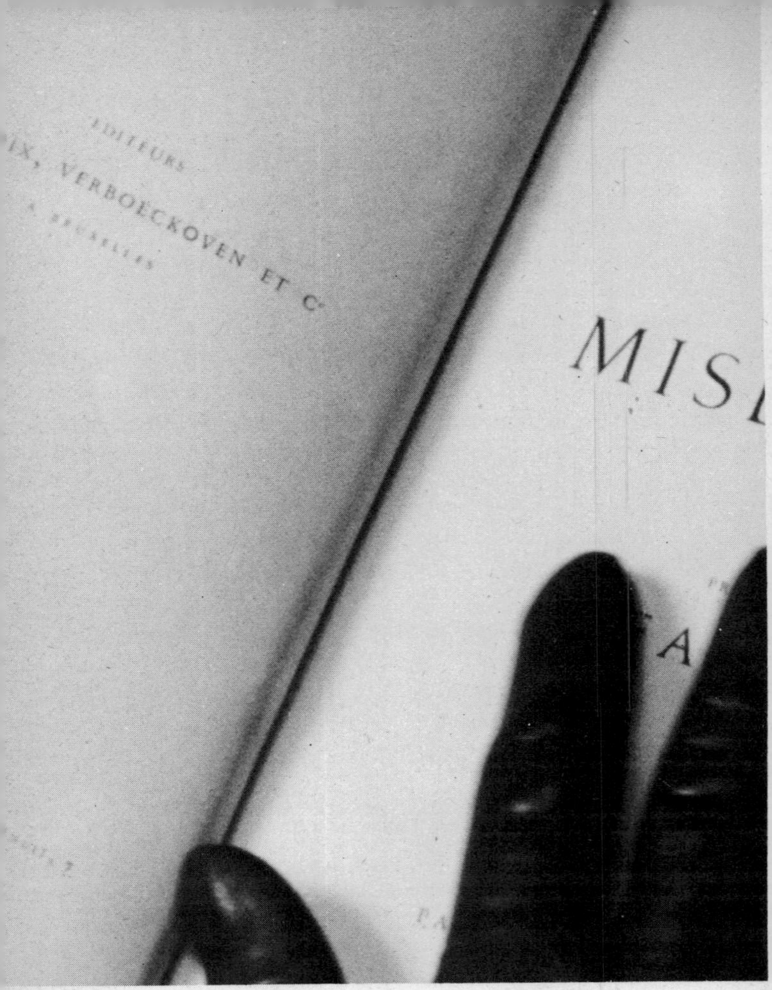
ÉDITEURS
VERBOECKOVEN ET C

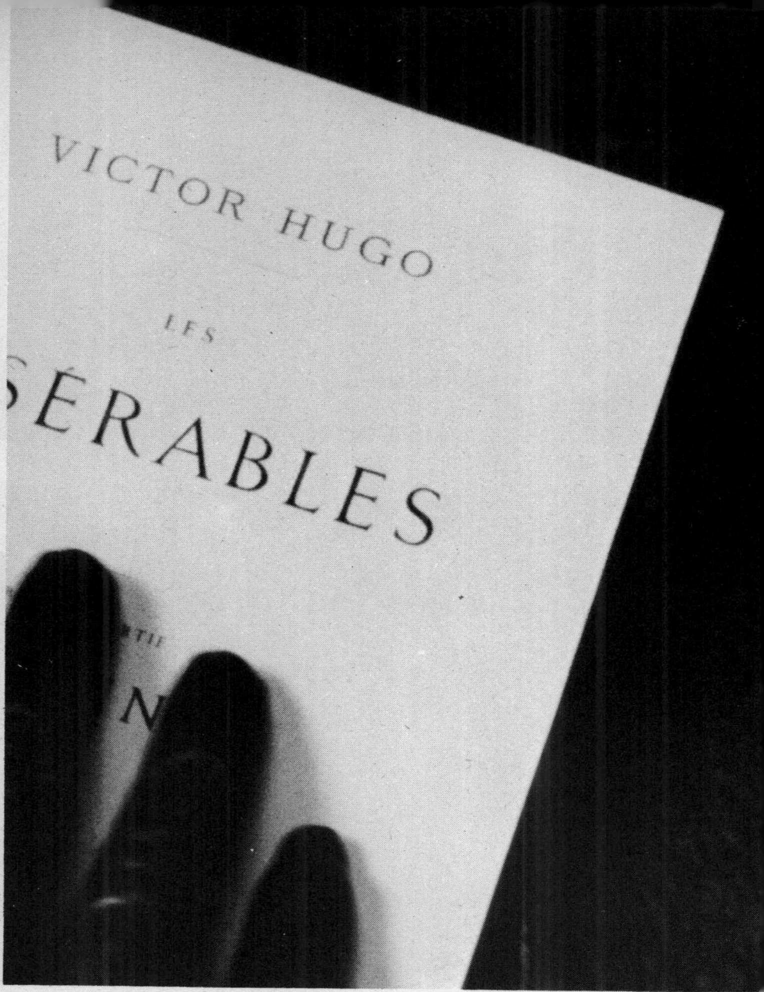
VICTOR HUGO
LES
SÉRABLES

*bound volumes. As she opens the first book, we see the
title:* Les Miserables *by Victor Hugo.*

ADELE *turns stiff and remains silent, her eyelids fluttering as she tries to control her shock.*

Disconcerted by her reaction, WHISTLER *begins to stammer in confusion.*

WHISTLER   I thought . . . I heard that . . .

ADELE   You heard nonsense and you listened to it. I will not be spied on!

Throwing some change on the counter, she picks up the ream of paper and angrily stalks toward the door.

ADELE   There must be another bookshop in town!

Crestfallen, WHISTLER *watches her leave.*

Fade out to black.

HALIFAX STREET. EXTERIOR. NIGHT.

From the men and women passing by, as well as from the action, we gather this is an area where the streetwalkers ply their trade. ADELE *walks up to one of the girls, speaks to her in a low tone of voice, then hands her a note and some money.*

STAIRCASE AND LANDING. INTERIOR. NIGHT.

The prostitute walks up a few steps and knocks at a door. PINSON *opens it and looks surprised as she hands him a note. As he reads it, we hear* ADELE'S *voice.*

ADELE'S VOICE   Albert my love,
I send you a young woman. Look at her. If you
find her to your taste, she will stay until morning.
You are so wonderful, my love, that you deserve all
the women on earth.
Accept my gift.

PINSON *looks up and stares thoughtfully at the prostitute.*

Fade out to black.

THEATRE. INTERIOR. NIGHT.

On the stage, a hypnotism act is under way. The
HYPNOTIST,[6] *a man of striking appearance and excep-*
tional self-confidence, is carefully instructing a Chinese
girl, apparently his assistant, to emerge from her trance.
From the rear of the balcony, we hear a voice raised in
protest. Unruffled, the performer invites the man to come
up to the stage. As the heckler rises to make his way for-
ward, we see that he is wearing a red uniform.

In reply to the HYPNOTIST's *question, the man identifies*
himself as RALPH WILLIAMS, *a member of the Mounted*
Police. Determined to expose the act as a fake, WILLIAMS
agrees to lend himself to an experiment. Meanwhile, on
the balcony, ADELE *leans forward to borrow the opera*
glasses of the woman in front of her. She uses them to
survey the rows of the orchestra, until she discovers PIN-
SON, *who is talking to a young woman in the next seat.*[7]

---

[6]The role of the hypnotist is played by Ivry Gitlis, the world-famous
violinist from Israel.
[7]Later on, we will discover that the young woman is his fiancée,
Agnes Johnstone.

On the stage, after successfully putting WILLIAMS *to sleep, the* HYPNOTIST *goes on to tell him that he is in a rowboat, on a beautiful lake, on a very hot day. Under his guidance,* WILLIAMS *rows harder and harder, gradually discarding his clothes. The* HYPNOTIST *now turns to the audience.*

HYPNOTIST   Mesdames, Mesdemoiselles, Messieurs. If I wanted to, I could force this man to leave the police and finish his life in a monastery.

Up on the balcony, ADELE, *obviously fascinated by the performance on stage, is scribbling in a small notebook.*

Satisfied that he has made his point, the HYPNOTIST *now proceeds to waken his recalcitrant subject.* WILLIAMS *regains consciousness, looks around in confusion, and begins to leave the stage, but the* HYPNOTIST *calls him back, reminding him to take his clothes.* WILLIAMS *grabs the bundle and scurries off the stage. To the sound of the audience's laughter and applause, the* HYPNOTIST *smilingly bows and makes his exit.*

BACKSTAGE. INTERIOR. NIGHT.

On the stairway leading to the dressing rooms, ADELE *carefully makes her way past several performers in costume. A juggler is practicing at the foot of the stairs. She stops at a door and knocks.*

DRESSING ROOM. INTERIOR. NIGHT.

The door is opened by the young Chinese assistant. Seated in front of a mirror, the HYPNOTIST *is wiping the make-up off his face. The assistant discreetly disappears behind a screen.*

ADELE   May I come in?

HYPNOTIST   Please do.

ADELE   I was in the theatre. I saw your performance. It was really remarkable. I was very impressed, but that's not why I came. I would like to propose a business transaction.

HYPNOTIST   I see. Do you run a theatre?

ADELE   No, it's something else.

HYPNOTIST   I'm listening . . . well, speak up!

ADELE   I am intrigued by your power.

HYPNOTIST   Thank you. I am only doing my job. I am merely the instrument of a mightier force from elsewhere.

ADELE   Are there limits to your power?

HYPNOTIST   Yes, indeed. Space, for instance: I cannot act on a subject outside of my presence . . . Tell me, are you a reporter?

ADELE   No, I would like to use your gifts for a personal matter.

HYPNOTIST   To cure a sick person?

ADELE   No.

HYPNOTIST   I've done that, you know.

ADELE   No, it's something else. Can you change a person's feelings?

HYPNOTIST   What do you mean?

ADELE   For instance, can you change love into hate. Or vice-versa?

HYPNOTIST   I'm sorry. I can act on the body, but not on the soul. All I can do through hypnosis is to

131

oblige certain people into acting against their will. I say certain people only because there are some subjects who do not respond.

ADELE Listen, could you compel a man to marry a woman?

HYPNOTIST Do you mean against his will?

ADELE Yes.

HYPNOTIST Well, maybe. Why not? Provided he can be lured to the proper place, with everything on hand for the ceremony. We would need a minister and two witnesses . . . I would say it isn't easy, but it is not impossible. It's simply a matter of money.

ADELE I've got money.

The HYPNOTIST *calls out to his assistant and says a few words in a foreign language.*[8] *She responds by hurrying out of the room. As soon as they are alone, the* HYPNOTIST *adopts a businesslike manner with his visitor.*

HYPNOTIST So, you've got money.

ADELE My father has!

HYPNOTIST Where is your father?

ADELE He lives in Europe. He is rich and famous.

HYPNOTIST In Europe, eh? Shall I write for him to send me the money?

ADELE No, his name must be kept out of this.

HYPNOTIST Listen, it just won't work. The matter is much too serious for me to rush into it blindly. Besides, why should I trust you? Who is your father?

---

[8]Gitlis speaks to the girl in Hebrew.

132

After a minute's hesitation, ADELE *responds to his question by slowly spelling out the name of* VICTOR HUGO *on a smoky mirror. As soon as he has registered the impact of her message,* ADELE *hastily wipes the name off the mirror with her gloved hand. The* HYPNOTIST *looks thoughtful as he speculates out loud.*

HYPNOTIST   Either you are not related to this man, in which case you'll never succeed in raising the amount of money I require . . . or else, you really are his daughter. In that case, it's a risky proposition and I'm not sure I can afford it.

ADELE   Then, you refuse?

HYPNOTIST   I refuse . . . unless . . . Look, I'll need five thousand francs, payable in advance.

ADELE   I'll have the money in a week.

HYPNOTIST   Fine! What we'll do is . . .

The conversation is interrupted by the abrupt entrance of a man dressed in worker's clothes and carrying a bundle of red clothes, which we recognize as RALPH WILLIAMS' *uniform.*

WILLIAMS   Excuse me, guv, where do I put this uniform? Over here?

ADELE's *eyes widen as she takes in the full impact of the vulgar hoax she has just narrowly escaped. Without a word, she walks out and runs up the stairs. Off-screen, we hear the sounds of an ugly dispute, with the* HYPNOTIST *beating his stooge and loudly berating him for his stupidity.*

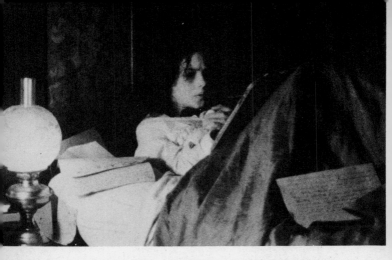

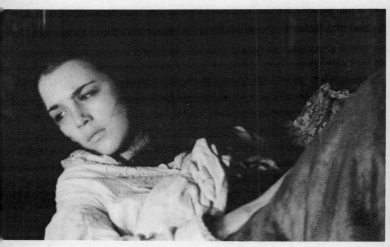

ADELE'S ROOM. INTERIOR. NIGHT.

Propped up against her bed pillows, ADELE *seems distraught as she scribbles feverishly.*

ADELE'S VOICE   I denounce the official records as a fraud of identity. Father unknown. I was born of an unknown father . . . Father completely unknown! If I was born with father unknown . . . then, I don't know my father.

Dropping her pen, she puts out the light. Gradually growing more frantic, she is clearly in great physical, as well as mental, anguish, as she goes on to mutter and to moan.

ADELE   The two newlyweds are buried together. Even death cannot part them . . . The dead young bride's dress is displayed in her parents' home . . . But, it's my home too! The bride's gown is displayed like a relic to all visitors. But what about me? What can I do? My eyes are burning . . . They hurt so much! I don't want to look at them . . . I don't want to see that trunk under the bed. Get rid of my sister's clothes! Burn them . . . give them away. I can't stand the sight of them! My eyes can't stand them . . .

SAUNDERS' STAIRCASE. INTERIOR. NIGHT.

Awakened by ADELE's *cries,* MRS. SAUNDERS *runs up the stairs and knocks at her door.*

MRS. SAUNDERS   Miss Adele, what's the matter? Let me in!

Fade out to black.

O'Brien's Coach. Interior and Exterior. Day.

Indicating that some time has elapsed, ADELE is now wearing glasses. She is reading a newspaper and visibly very upset by an item she reads over and over, as she mutters out loud.

ADELE How can he do this? He can't do this! Johnstone . . . Agnes Johnstone!

Now, she cries out to the coachman.

ADELE O'Brien, do you know Mount Amelia Manor?
O'BRIEN Yes, Miss Lewly.
ADELE Take me there.

O'BRIEN pulls the horse to a halt and turns around. The vehicle moves off in the opposite direction.

Mount Amelia. Exterior. Day.

The coach comes to a stop in front of a vast, colonial-style residence. After instructing O'BRIEN to wait, ADELE gets out, walks over to the stoop, and rings the bell.

The Entrance Hall at Mount Amelia. Interior. Day.

An elderly male servant opens the door. ADELE asks to speak to JUDGE JOHNSTONE. He tries to prevent her from entering, explaining that the JUDGE sees visitors only by appointment. She pushes her way in and, in a loud voice, insists on seeing the JUDGE immediately.

AGNES JOHNSTONE, *standing on a balcony overlooking the entrance hall, volunteers to arrange for her father to see the visitor.*

As she comes down the stairs, we recognize her as the young girl we have seen previously, sitting next to PINSON *during the* HYPNOTIST's *performance at the theatre. The girl enters the* JUDGE's *office and emerges a few minutes later, telling* ADELE *that her father will see her. Ignoring* AGNES' *gracious gesture,* ADELE *sweeps past her on her way into the office.*

OFFICE IN MOUNT AMELIA. INTERIOR. DAY.

The JUDGE *courteously greets* ADELE *as she enters and offers her a seat.*

ADELE Thank you, sir, for agreeing to see me when you don't know who I am.

JUDGE You're French, aren't you?

ADELE Yes, I am the daughter of Victor Hugo.

JUDGE The writer? I don't share his political views, but I admire his courage.

ADELE Sir, I'll come straight to the point. I've just read of your daughter's engagement. I must advise you that Lieutenant Pinson is unworthy of your family.

JUDGE That's a very serious allegation.

ADELE I'm well aware of it. I've known Lieutenant Pinson for several years. He was shrewd enough to ingratiate himself with my family. He courted me discreetly, but persistently, and I admit that I responded to his courtship. After two years of exile, I

143

144

had little experience of the world and I was lonely. He took every advantage of my naïveté. I became so infatuated that I broke off my engagement with Monsieur Auguste Vacquerie, a friend of my father. I was determined to marry Lieutenant Pinson.

JUDGE   But your parents . . .

ADELE   They strongly objected to our marriage. My mother, who suspected I was meeting Pinson in secret, undertook to look up his past: he is not a vicar's son, as he claims. He was sentenced for unpaid debts and given a choice between prison and the army. He choose the army. However, in the face of my determination, my parents finally gave their consent and our marriage took place. Lieutenant Pinson even signed the contract.

JUDGE   Have you any proof of all this?

ADELE   Certainly, I have it with me. Here are the announcements of our engagement and our wedding that were printed by the Guernsey press. I also have my parents' written consent to our marriage.

JUDGE   If Pinson is as bad as you say, how can you still be his wife?

ADELE   Do you think we can control our emotions? One can be in love with a man and yet be aware that he is utterly despicable. Besides, there's something else . . .

ADELE *rises with a significant look.*

ADELE   I'm expecting his child.

From the JUDGE's *stare, we understand she is showing him her swollen stomach.*

COUNTRYSIDE. EXTERIOR. DAY.

From a distance, ADELE is following some cavalrymen on their cross-country maneuvers. She proceeds along a path concealed by hedgerows and overlooking the sea, along which some twenty men are riding, under PINSON's command.

ADELE comes closer, until she blocks PINSON's passage. Facing him, she holds up a roll of banknotes. Ignoring her offer, he simply stares down at her. She lets the bills drop from her hand, allowing them to drift away like leaves in the wind.

Now, she removes a cushion from under her dress and tosses it in his direction. He reacts to her gesture with cold contempt.

PINSON   You're ridiculous!

He calls out a command to his men and spurs his horse in their direction.

MOUNT AMELIA MANOR. EXTERIOR. DAY.

PINSON's carriage stops in front of the JUDGE's house. He gets out and goes to the door and rings. Instead of letting him in, the elderly servant we have seen before blocks his way.

PINSON   Evening, George.

GEORGE   Miss Agnes is not at home, sir.

PINSON   But she's expecting me. We're going to the opera.

GEORGE   Miss Agnes is not at home.

PINSON   Well, let me come in. I'll have a word with the Judge.

GEORGE   The Judge is not at home, sir.

PINSON   But his carriage is in the drive.

GEORGE   I'm very sorry, sir. There's no one at home.

GEORGE *firmly closes the door, leaving* PINSON *outside.*

THE BARRACKS. PINSON'S QUARTERS. INTERIOR. DAY.

PINSON's *uniform is covered with dust from the country maneuvers. Worn out from the heat, the sweat, the dust, he is also still seething as he winds up his account of* ADELE's *latest outrage to his orderly.*

PINSON   I intend to have that woman deported. To hell with the scandal!

Brushing off PINSON's *uniform,* HATHWELL *tries to soothe his frayed nerves.*

HATHWELL   Oh, come now, Lieutenant. Calm down; there is a way. I've never given you bad advice, have I?

PINSON   I'm listening.

HATHWELL   Well, if I've got it right, all this woman has to do is to leave Halifax and your troubles are over.

PINSON   Yes, but how do I get her to leave? I've tried everything: prayers . . . promises . . . Nothing works!

HATHWELL   Well, since she follows you around like a little dog, she'll never leave Halifax until you do.

PINSON   Thank you very much. That's a big help. There's no question of me leaving.

HATHWELL   Well, sir, I've heard differently. There's a rumor going around the barracks that the regiment might be sent away very soon.

The camera moves in on PINSON, *leaving* HATHWELL *out of the image.*

ADELE'S ROOM. INTERIOR. NIGHT.

With MRS. SAUNDERS' *help,* ADELE *is finishing her packing.*

MRS. SAUNDERS   We shall miss you, but you've made the right decision. And I know that your parents will be so happy to see you again, after all this time. I hope . . . I mean . . . about Lieutenant Pinson. I hope you've put him out of your mind. He's not worthy of you! Who does he think he is . . . refusing to marry you!

ADELE   You're wrong, Mrs. Saunders. I was the one who refused to marry. I think marriage is degrading for a woman, particularly for a woman like me. My work requires solitude. Besides, think of my name, Mrs. Saunders. Think of who my father is. I would never give up the name of Mademoiselle Hugo.

MRS. SAUNDERS   Of course, I understand.

MRS. SAUNDERS *leaves the room. After bolting the door behind her,* ADELE *goes over to the closet, removes a picture of* PINSON *that is hidden there and carefully puts it in her suitcase.*

Visibly worn and discouraged, ADELE *stands there for a moment, brooding. Now the camera, establishing a moving contrast between present and past, travels back in time and space to superimpose the radiant vision of a much younger* ADELE *in Guernsey: the young girl, standing on a rock by the sea and facing the waves, has a hopeful, faraway look in her eyes as she contemplates the future.*

YOUNG ADELE'S VOICE   This incredible thing—that a girl who today begs her father for her daily bread, would come into her own within four years—this, I shall accomplish. This incredible thing—that a young girl shall walk over the sea, from the Old into the New World, to join her lover—this, I shall accomplish.

The Saunders' Parlor. Interior. Evening.

Her bags packed, ADELE *is ready to leave.* MRS. SAUNDERS *goes over to her with a farewell gift.*

MRS. SAUNDERS   Miss Adele, I have a present for you. It's a cape, much too fine for me. It will look lovely on you. Keep it to remember us by.

Visibly moved, ADELE *thanks the older woman profusely. In a warm gesture, she reaches out to caress* MRS. SAUNDERS *and embraces her affectionately.*

As she leaves, MRS. SAUNDERS *stands in the doorway.*

MRS. SAUNDERS   Write to us when you get home.

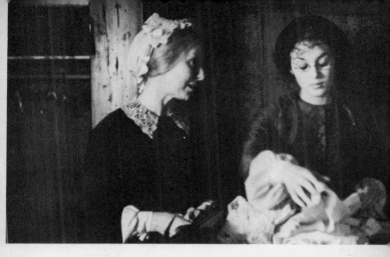

O'BRIEN'S COACH. INTERIOR. NIGHT.

Once inside the coach, ADELE, unable to contain her despair, bursts into tears. Throughout the scene, she sobs uncontrollably.

O'BRIEN   Where to, Miss?

ADELE   I don't know. I don't know any more.

O'BRIEN   Why don't you stay with Mrs. Saunders a few days longer?

ADELE   I can't. I don't want to see her again!

O'BRIEN   Shall we go to the hotel?

ADELE   I have no money left.

O'BRIEN   Well . . . I do know of a place where you won't have to pay.

Fade out to black.

A WOMEN'S SHELTER. INTERIOR. DAYBREAK.

The row of beds inside a vast dormitory indicates that it is a refuge for destitute women. As the camera sweeps through the dormitory toward ADELE asleep in bed, we see that the other inmates are considerably older than she is. The woman in the next bed is awake, eying ADELE's suitcase on the floor. Finally, she leans over, reaches out for it, and lifts the cover to pick up a book. Just then, ADELE wakes up and slams the lid down on the thief's fingers.

ADELE   Don't touch that. It's my book!

The woman retreats. ADELE now moves over to the other side of the bed, slides to the ground and under the bed and over to her property. Her head against the suitcase, she settles down to sleep.

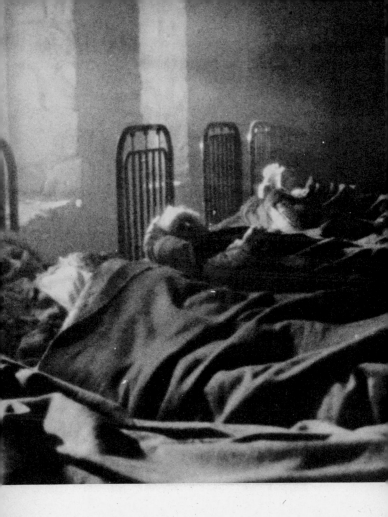

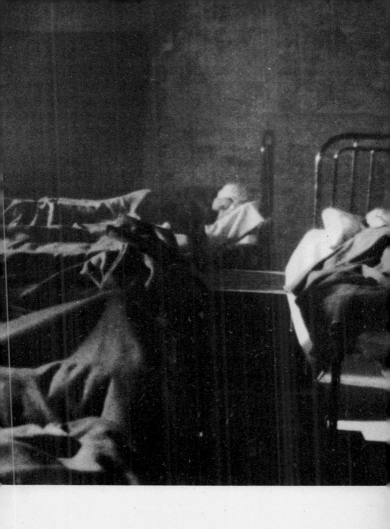

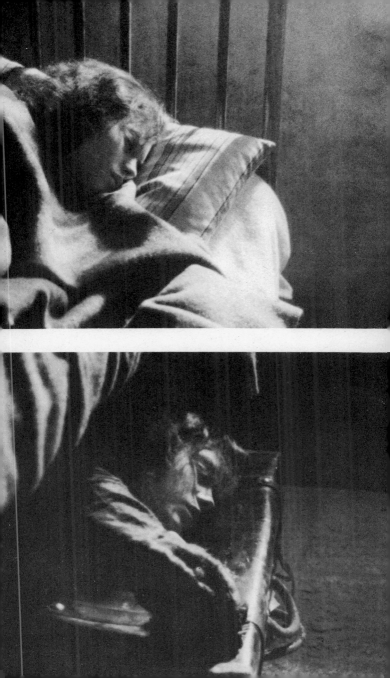

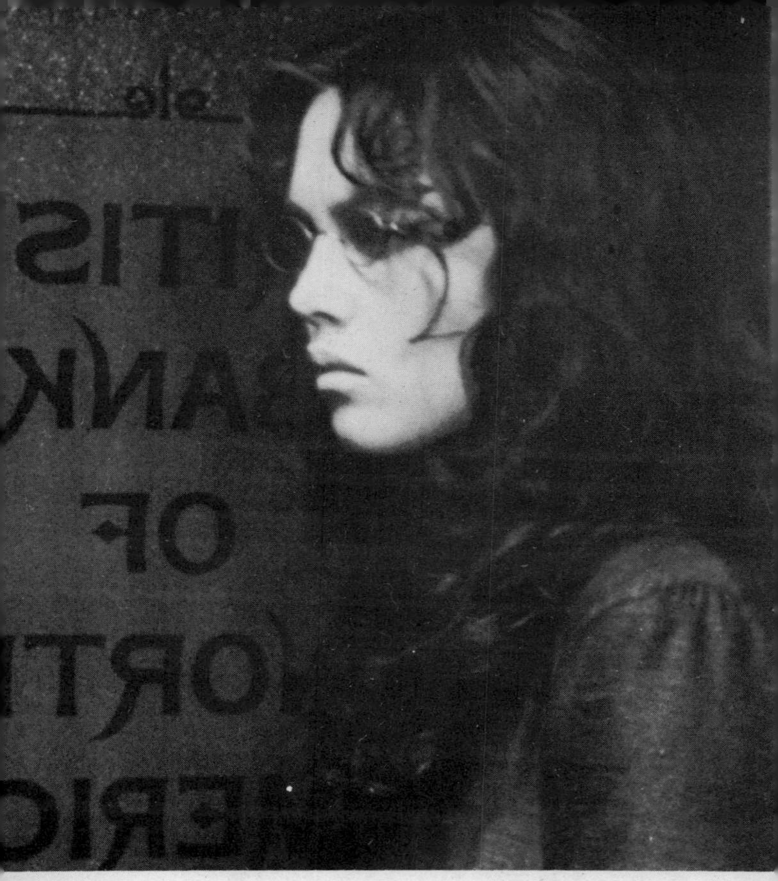

THE HALIFAX BANK. INTERIOR. DAY.

ADELE's rundown appearance, as well as her odd behavior, suggests that some time has elapsed since we last saw her: thinner and haggard, she mutters to herself as she walks up to counter to ask for her mail. The clerk fails to recognize her, but upon her insistence, he moves away to query two of his colleagues about the strange woman. They are both equally negative.

At his point, the clerk who has handled all her past transactions steps out of his office. His manner is sympathetic as he apologizes for his colleagues, explaining that they are new employees. After searching through a stack of envelopes, he hands her a letter.

VOICE OF VICTOR HUGO   Adele,
Here are seven hundred francs for your return passage. If you persist in staying in Halifax, despite our promises, this amount will be deducted from your pension. You complain we are slow in arranging to have your music published. You should realize that, for the time being, it is best to avoid attracting attention to yourself. Your mother is so ill that we keep your letters from her so as not to aggravate her condition. She has left Guernsey to settle in Brussels. I am now alone in Hauteville House.
Adele, my dear daughter, I await you with open arms. I am old. My greatest joy would be to have you all by my side.

PINSON'S QUARTERS. INTERIOR. DAY.

Intrigued by the fierce barking of a dog in the street, PINSON looks out of his window. He sees ADELE, her

BRUSSELS
We learned of the death of Mrs. Victor Hugo wife of the world famous French writer.

Wills, &c.; Churches; Licensed Chapels; Fees for Licenses; English and French Dissenting Chapels; Government Post-office and Postmen; Mails made up in London; Steam Packet List; Mails to India,

BRITISH TROOP MOVEMENTS

We hereby announce that the 16th Hussars, stationed in Halifax, will be moving on the 15th February, 1864 to the Barbados Islands.

Customs; Marine Insurance Agents; Consuls; Physicians; Surgeons; Dentists; Druggists; Veterinary Surgeons; Fire Engine Establishment; Public Agents;

dirty clothing and unkempt hair giving her the appear-
ance of a derelict, cringing in fear of the dog who is
attacking her. The frightened young woman turns
around and begins to run up the cobblestone street, with
the dog, in close pursuit, still yapping and jumping at her
heels. As she moves off in the distance, we see that the
bottom of her long silk gown is torn to shreds.

WHISTLER'S BOOKSHOP. INTERIOR. DAY.

WHISTLER, looking out, sees ADELE passing by on the
street, talking to herself and gesticulating wildly. As he
registers the evidence of her mental and physical deterior-
ation, the expression on his face suggests that his compas-
sion is tinged by a feeling of nostalgic longing.

THE MARKET PLACE. EXTERIOR. DAY.

MRS. SAUNDERS makes her way through the colorful food
stalls and stops to make her choice at a fruit and vegetable
stand. ADELE comes into view, wandering aimlessly and
still talking to herself. As she espies MRS. SAUNDERS, she
stops in alarm, then moves furtively around the stall until
she is safely out of sight.

HALIFAX STREET. EXTERIOR. DAY.

A little further on, a group of people are standing in front
of a bulletin board displaying the daily paper. ADELE
passes by, oblivious to the object of their curiosity. The
camera moves in, closing up on one of the printed items.
We read: BRUSSELS. MME VICTOR HUGO,
WIFE OF THE GREAT FRENCH WRITER, IS
DEAD.

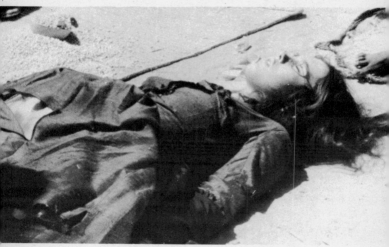

As the camera sweeps upward, we read a second notice:
BRITISH TROOPS MOVE OUT: ACCORDING
TO AN OFFICIAL ANNOUNCEMENT, THE
16TH HUSSARS REGIMENT, STATIONED IN
HALIFAX, WILL TRANSFER TO THE BAR-
BADOS ISLANDS. THEY ARE SCHEDULED
TO LEAVE ON FEBRUARY 15, 1864.

SQUARE IN BRIDGETOWN. EXTERIOR. DAY.

*The bright sunshine, the animated, noisy crowds of na-
tives in colorful attire, the vendors hawking their wares,
indicate a tropical locale that contrasts sharply with the
sober atmosphere of Halifax.* ADELE, *in her heavy
threadbare gown, is a strange and pathetic figure as she
wearily makes her way through the square, a mob of howl-
ing children at her heels. Impervious to their taunts, as
well as to the heat, she is clearly immersed in a world of
her own. Suddenly, she stops, puts her hand to her
forehead, and falls to the ground. A crowd gathers
around her. Now, a stout old black woman with white
hair pushes her way through the crowd. She chases the
children away.*

MME BAA   Leave the French lady alone!

*With the help of a servant, she lifts the young woman to
her feet. With* ADELE *leaning against her,* MME BAA
*steers her toward her house. As the camera moves back, we
now discover that* HATHWELL, PINSON'S *orderly, has
observed the whole scene.*

A GARDEN PARTY IN BRIDGETOWN. EXTERIOR.
DAY.

HATHWELL *makes his way through the festive gathering, looking for* PINSON. *He finds him on an upper terrace, talking to a lovely young woman.*

HATHWELL   Excuse me, Mrs. Pinson. I must have a word with the Captain.

MRS. PINSON   Of course!

The two men move aside.

HATHWELL   There's something you should know: I was in the Negro quarter this morning. At the market place, I saw a European woman causing quite a scene. I got near her and it was her: Miss Hugo!

PINSON   What?

HATHWELL   Yes, and I have worse news than that: she is going by the name of Mrs. Pinson!

PINSON   We've got to find her. What happened in Halifax must not happen here!

His wife goes over to join him.

MRS. PINSON   What's the matter, Albert?

PINSON   Oh, it's nothing, my dear . . .

MME BAA'S HOUSE. EXTERIOR. DAY.

ADELE *is lying in bed on the veranda. Feverish and highly agitated, she seems to be suffocating. We now see that* MME BAA *is by her side, nursing her. As she applies a cold, wet compress to her face, the sick girl gratefully kisses the old woman's hand.*

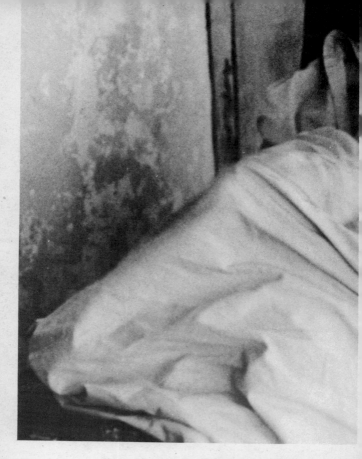

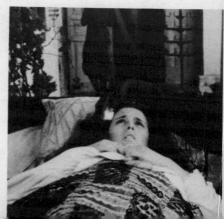

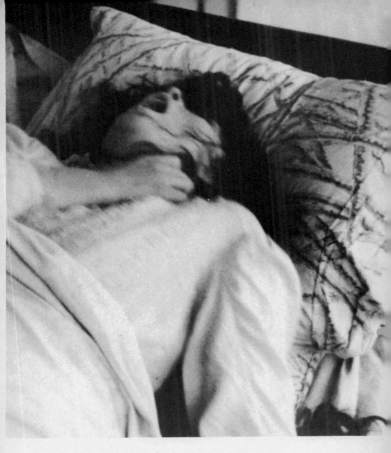

Streets in Bridgetown. Exterior. Day.

Wearing MRS. SAUNDERS' *heavy black cape over her tattered dress, her hair wildly disheveled,* ADELE *is slowly wandering through the streets, strangely detached from her environment. We now see that* PINSON *and* HATHWELL *have been observing her. Leaving his orderly behind,* PINSON *starts to follow the girl, keeping some distance between them as she pursues her erratic course, with apparently no specific destination in mind.*

After a while, he quickens his pace to catch up with her and stops a few feet away. ADELE *now turns her eyes in his direction, gives him a blank stare, and, without breaking her pace, walks past him.*

PINSON *calls out to her.*

PINSON   Adele.

She doesn't respond. He now runs in front of her and, again, calls out her name.

PINSON   Adele!

He seems bewildered as ADELE, *looking straight ahead, takes no notice and keeps on walking until she finally disappears around a corner.*

Like PINSON, *we can only wonder whether she has recognized her former lover, or even seen him. But we may imagine that* ADELE *has at last been liberated from her obsession.*

MME BAA'S HOUSE. EXTERIOR. DAY.

Seated on her veranda, MME BAA *has just finished dictating a letter to the local* SCRIBE:

SCRIBE   I'll read the letter over to you. I've changed it a little and you can tell me whether it's all right: "Sir, I am a simple woman from Barbados Island. But though I never learned to read, I know the name of Victor Hugo. Ten years ago, I was still a slave and I know that you are a defender of the oppressed.

In the streets of Bridgetown, I had noticed a strange-looking young woman, who seemed to be in great distress. The children ran after her and taunted her. It was so pitiful that I decided to protect her. I brought her home and nursed her. I learned that she is your daughter and that she was deserted by an officer she followed first to Halifax and then here, to Barbados.

Sorrow has broken her body and soul. The body may heal, but the soul is probably lost. Adele must return to her country and to the warmth of her family. If you wish, Monsieur Victor Hugo, I can bring your daughter back to Europe. Monsieur Werder, of Martinique, will advance the money for our journey."

As the camera leaves the SCRIBE *and* MME BAA *to track along the veranda, we see a superimposed image of* ADELE *leaning on* MME BAA *and walking forward. On this image, we hear the* NARRATOR *begin his final commentary.*

NARRATOR   And so, Adele returned to France with Mme Baa.

The rest of the commentary unfolds over a series of photographic documents that illustrate his words.

First, we see an engraving showing VICTOR HUGO *being hailed by the crowds on his return from exile.*

NARRATOR   Major changes had taken place in Europe. Following the fall of Napoleon III, Victor Hugo returned to Paris, after eighteen years of exile.

(Over a picture of the clinic at St. Mande:)

NARRATOR   Reunited with his daughter Adele, he placed her in a clinic at St. Mande. She lived there for forty years, gardening, playing the piano . . .

(Over a flashback image of the manuscript of her diary:)

NARRATOR   . . . and writing her diary in code. Adele survived her whole family.

(Over a picture of VICTOR HUGO *on his death bed:)*

NARRATOR   Her father died on May 22nd, 1885. His last words were: "I see a black light."

Fade out to black.

(A picture showing the huge throngs following his funeral procession:)

NARRATOR   The day of Victor Hugo's funeral was a day of mourning for all of France.

(A picture showing the huge crowds at the Arch of Triumph:)

NARRATOR   His body lay in state all night, under the Arch of Triumph.

(A picture of huge throngs gathered in front of the Pantheon:)

NARRATOR   And the next day, two million Parisians followed his coffin from there to the Pantheon.

(A picture of ADELE's *grave, beside that of her mother. Just behind is the grave of Leopoldine and her husband:)*

NARRATOR   Adele's death, in 1915, went almost unnoticed in the turmoil of World War I, then raging in Europe.

THE GUERNSEY COAST. EXTERIOR. DAY.

We now go back to the image of the young girl standing on a rock by the sea, proclaiming her faith in the future.

NARRATOR   Fifty years earlier, Adele had written in her diary . . .

ADELE'S VOICE   That a young girl shall walk over the sea, from the Old into the New World, to join her lover—this, I shall accomplish.

The camera closes in on the girl: young ADELE's *face remains on the screen, while the final credits unfold over her radiant image.*